Poké Rap!

I want to be the very best there ever was
To beat all the rest, yeah, that's my cause

Catch 'em, Catch 'em, Gotta catch 'em all

Pokémon I'll search across the land
Look far and wide
Release from my hand
The power that's inside

Catch 'em, Catch 'em, Gotta catch 'em all Pokémon!

Gotta catch 'em all, Gotta catch 'em all
Gotta catch 'em all, Gotta catch 'em all

At least one hundred and fifty or more to see
To be a Pokémon Master is my destiny

Catch 'em, Catch 'em, Gotta catch 'em all
Gotta catch 'em all, Pokémon! (repeat three times)

Can YOU Rap all 150?

Here's the rest of the Poké Rap.

Dratini, Growlithe, Mr. Mime, Cubone
Graveler, Voltorb, Gloom

Charmeleon, Wartortle
Mewtwo, Tentacruel, Aerodactyl
Omanyte, Slowpoke
Pidgeot, Arbok
That's all folks!

Words and Music by Tamara Loeffler and John Siegler
Copyright © 1999 Pikachu Music (BMI)
Worldwide rights for Pikachu Music administered by Cherry River Music Co. (BMI)
All Rights Reserved   Used by Permission

Collect them all!

Pokémon

Battle for the Zephyr Badge

All rights reserved. Published by Scholastic Inc., *Publishers since 1920*. SCHOLASTIC and associated logos are trademarks and/or registered trademarks of Scholastic Inc.

The publisher does not have any control over and does not assume any responsibility for author or third-party websites or their content.

This book is a work of fiction. Names, characters, places, and incidents are either the product of the author's imagination or are used fictitiously, and any resemblance to actual persons, living or dead, business establishments, events, or locales is entirely coincidental.

ISBN 978-1-338-28406-5

10 9 8 7 6 5 4 3 2   18 19 20 21 22

Printed in the U.S.A.   40
First printing 2018

Battle for the Zephyr Badge

Adapted by Jennifer Johnson

Scholastic Inc.

The GS Ball Thief

"Thanks, Pikachu. We'll have the best looking Poké Balls at the Violet City Gym," said Ash Ketchum.

Ash and his yellow Electric-type Pokémon, Pikachu, were in the beautiful gardens of Cherrygrove City. Ash was polishing his Poké Balls beside a river. Pikachu was helping. As Ash set down the last of several gleaming red-and-white Poké Balls, Pikachu handed him one more ball.

It was different from the other Poké Balls. This special gold-and-silver Poké Ball was called the GS Ball. Professor Oak, a Pokémon expert, had sent Ash all the way to the Orange Islands to get it.

But Professor Oak couldn't open the mysterious Poké
Ball. So he sent Ash and his friends on another mission
to the western territories. He wanted Ash to find Kurt,
the man who designed the GS Ball. Professor Oak hoped
Kurt could open the ball and find out what was inside.

Ash was glad for the opportunity. As soon as Ash
arrived in the western territories, he headed straight
to New Bark Town to sign up for the Johto League. He
might as well test his skills and earn some badges as
long as he was on a journey. If he earned eight badges at
eight different Johto League gyms, Ash could compete
in the Johto League Tournament, and show off his skills
as a Pokémon Trainer. At the moment, Ash was on his

way to the Violet City Gym to compete for his very first Johto League badge.

It seemed like ages ago since Ash had first got the GS Ball. And now they were way out west, far away from home and Professor Oak. Sunlight sparkled on the GS Ball as Ash polished it.

Ash's friend Misty watched him work. "Ash, you need more than shiny Poké Balls to win at the Violet City Gym," she teased. "You need to practice your skills as a Pokémon Trainer."

Ash ignored the teasing. But he knew what Misty meant. Gym battles were the toughest competitions a Trainer could face. He had to be ready.

A delicious smell wafted through the air. "Brock's cooking lunch," Misty said.

Ash's friend Brock was a former Gym Leader. He traveled with Ash and Misty.

Ash put the GS Ball on the ground and watched his friends. She had orange hair and carried around a small Spike Ball Pokémon, Togepi. Togepi's tiny arms, legs, and head stuck out of the eggshell it had hatched from.

Brock was stirring something over a small fire. It smelled great.

"It's ready," he called, holding up his cooking pan. Misty and Ash raced to the campfire to join Brock. But their lunch was interrupted before it began.

"Pika!" From a spot on the riverbank, Pikachu let out a startled cry.

Ash whirled around.

"Huh?"

Pikachu pointed to something in the river. A shiny blue Pokémon had popped up from underwater. It had a big, thick tail, like a paddle.

Ash was always excited to run into a new breed of Pokémon. He hurried to the river and pulled

out Dexter, his Pokédex. The tiny computer held information about all the world's Pokémon. "What is that?" Ash asked.

"Quagsire. A Water-type Pokémon." Dexter replied. "Quagsire inhabits pure-water lakes. Its skin is covered with a special slippery layer, making it very difficult to catch."

Misty was excited, too. She was crazy about Water-type Pokémon. "With that slick look, Quagsire's really cool!"

"*Quagsire.*" The Quagsire's voice was soft and quiet.

"All right!" Misty shouted. "I'm going to catch it." She pulled a Poké Ball from her backpack and threw it as hard as she could.

"*Psyduck.*" An orange Pokémon popped out.

Ash groaned. Instead of going after Quagsire, it just stood there and stared.

Misty raced over to Psyduck.

"This is useless," Misty said. She scooped up the Pokémon in her arms.

As she lifted Psyduck, Misty accidentally kicked the GS Ball. It rolled down the river bank toward Quagsire.

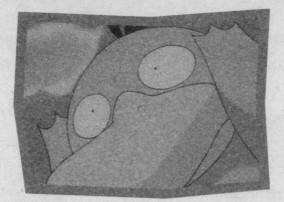

"Quagsire!" Quick as a flash, the slippery blue Pokémon grabbed the GS Ball in its mouth and swam away.

Ash couldn't believe his eyes. "Hey, hold on! Bring back the GS Ball!" Ash grabbed a Poké Ball and raced down the riverbank after Quagsire, with Pikachu right behind him. Puffing and panting, Ash tossed a Poké Ball into the river. "Help me out, Squirtle."

Squirtle exploded from the ball. It had a blue body and a hard shell. It swam after Quagsire as fast as it could. When it was pretty close, Squirtle took a flying leap and landed on Quagsire's back.

"Good work, Squirtle!" Ash called. "Now grab that GS Ball."

Squirtle tried to get the ball out of Quagsire's mouth. But Quagsire's skin was too slippery. Squirtle couldn't hold on.

Quagsire knew it had the advantage. It ducked down and threw Squirtle off its back. Squirtle flew high over Quagsire's head. *Splash!* Squirtle landed on its back in the water. Quagsire raced on past.

"Are you all right?" Ash shouted.

"Squirtle!" The Pokémon flipped over and chased after Quagsire. It jumped into the air and tried to land on Quagsire again. But Quagsire used its thick tail to swat Squirtle. Once again, Squirtle flew into the air and splash-landed on its back.

"Squirtle, don't give up!" Ash shouted. "Water Gun!"

Squirtle flipped over and squirted a huge jet of water at Quagsire's head. Quagsire opened its mouth so it could return the attack. Out popped the GS Ball! The gold-and-silver ball sailed high into the air.

"Pika!" Pikachu reached over the water and caught the GS Ball.

Ash breathed a sigh of relief. "Nice work!"

In the river, Squirtle aimed another jet of water at Quagsire. The slippery Pokémon had a Water Gun attack of its own. It fired a stream right back at Squirtle. The two jets of water collided in midair.

Misty still wanted to capture Quagsire. She grabbed

a Poké Ball from her backpack and got ready to throw. "Okay, Quagsire, you're mi-"

The shrill sound of a police whistle cut off Misty's cry. Ash, Misty, and Brock turned around. A blue-haired police officer was sitting on a motorcycle. She did not look happy.

Ash and the others recognized the officer right away. Every town Ash had visited had a police officer named Jenny.

This Officer Jenny dangled a pair of shiny silver handcuffs from her fingers.

"You're all under arrest!" she said.

2

The Quagsire That Wouldn't Give Up

"Under arrest?" Ash asked.

"This area is a Quagsire preservation," Officer Jenny said. "You can't catch Quagsire here."

Ash and the others tried to explain that they didn't know about the preservation. Officer Jenny took them down to her headquarters so she could check out the story with Professor Oak. She called up the professor on a videophone. His face appeared on the screen.

Professor Oak explained, "The Quagsire in Cherrygrove City will only live in very clean waters.

The townspeople are able to tell if local water is pure by whether or not Quagsire live there."

Officer Jenny turned to Ash, Misty, and Brock. "From now on, you must not raise a finger against a Quagsire," she said. "That means no capturing or even battling. Do you understand?"

"Yes," Ash and his friends replied all together.

Ash said good-bye to Professor Oak and turned to Officer Jenny. "One thing still seems strange. Why did the Quagsire try to take this?" He held out the GS Ball.

"Because it's round," Officer Jenny said.

"Huh?" Her answer made no sense to Ash.

"The Quagsire of Cherrygrove City are said to live at Blue Moon Falls," Jenny explained. "Quagsire begin to appear in town around this time every year. They take any round objects that strike their fancy. Then they swim back upstream. The next day many of the round objects the Quagsire took come floating down the river and return to their owners."

"They come back?" Ash was glad to hear it. He didn't plan to lose the GS Ball again – but just in case.

"They come back carrying pure water and good luck with them," Officer Jenny replied. "At least, that's what we've always said here in Cherrygrove City. They say the last object to come floating back is the luckiest of all."

Then Officer Jenny turned to the window. "What's that?" she asked.

Something was rapping on the window pane.

"Quagsire!" Misty shouted.

The blue Water-type Pokémon stared at them through the glass.

"It's the one we just saw," Ash said.

"I'll bet it's still after the GS Ball," Brock guessed.

"Pika," Pikachu chimed in.

"Quagsire, quag, quag!" Quagsire was definitely staring at the GS Ball.

"No, you can't have it," Ash said sternly.

"*Quagsire*," the Pokémon said. It slid down and disappeared below the windowsill.

Ash was relieved. He couldn't risk losing the GS Ball again.

"We'd better get to the next town," Ash said. Misty and Brock agreed. They said good-bye to Officer Jenny and headed out.

Soon they were crossing a bridge over the river. Ash looked down at the blue water.

"*Pika*." Pikachu sounded worried.

Ash looked down at Pikachu. Quagsire was back! It was sitting right beside Pikachu on the bridge.

The Quagsire stretched its arms out toward Ash. "*Quagsire*."

Ash couldn't believe it. This Quagsire just wouldn't give up.

Quagsire took a flying leap and landed right on top of Ash.

"Hey, knock it off!" Ash turned left and then right, trying to shake off Quagsire. But the Pokémon hung on tight.

"Somebody, do something!" Ash yelled.

Brock and Misty tried to pull Quagsire off Ash. But their hands slid right off Quagsire's slippery back.

Finally, Ash managed to pull a Poké Ball from his backpack. He cocked his arm and tossed it past Quagsire.

"Chika!" Chikorita, a small Grass-type Pokémon, popped out. The light green Pokémon had a ring of dark green spots around its neck. Chikorita also had a long, pointy green leaf growing from the top of its head.

Chikorita glared at Quagsire. The leaf on its head began to spin like a propeller. Chikorita rose into the air and whirled toward Ash and Quagsire. The gust of wind it created blew Quagsire away.

The little Grass-type Pokémon landed gently in front of Ash.

Suddenly, Ash felt something behind him. Quagsire was back!

"Chika!" Once again, the Grass-type Pokémon used its propeller. It whirled toward Quagsire, trying to blow it away. Instead, it almost blew Ash right off the bridge. Ash's backpack flew off his back.

"Quit it, Chikorita!" Ash said.

Ash's backpack flapped open in the breeze. The wind picked up the GS Ball and sent it flying out of the backpack.

Quickly, Quagsire dove at the flying GS Ball. It caught the ball in its wide mouth. Quagsire leaped over the bridge's railing and landed in the river. Then Quagsire swam away.

"Oh, no!" Ash yelled. "It's got the GS Ball again!"

A Slippery Capture

"Where could that Quagsire have gone?" Ash asked.

Ash, Pikachu, Misty, and Brock had raced along the riverbank until they were all out of breath. Now they were standing on a wooden bridge over the river. Behind them, the sun was setting. Quagsire was nowhere to be seen.

"Quagsire swam up the river," Brock said. "It's got to be here somewhere."

Misty looked annoyed. "Don't you think we'd be better off waiting back in town than wandering around aimlessly?"

Brock considered this. "Misty's right. If we're lucky,

the GS Ball should come back downstream."

"But what if we're not lucky?" Ash asked. He remembered what Officer Jenny had said. The Quagsire were supposed to return all the round objects. But Ash wasn't sure he trusted that story.

Then Pikachu started to jump up and down. *"Pika! Pika pi!"*

"What's the matter, Pikachu?" Ash asked. He looked down at the river.

"Hey, it's Quagsire!" he shouted. Not one, not two, but four of the slippery Pokémon were swimming past. All of the Quagsire were carrying round items. But none of them had the GS Ball.

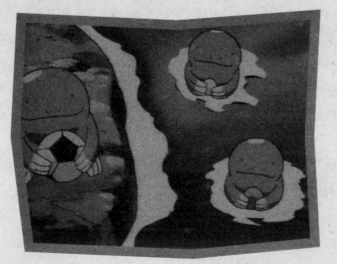

That didn't seem to worry Brock. "I'll bet anything they're going to meet their friends," he said.

"All right, let's go!" Ash took off in the direction the Quagsire were swimming. Misty and Brock trailed right behind him. They followed the Quagsire up the river.

After a while, the river ran into a large pool. Ash and the others hid in some reeds at the edge of the water. They parted the reeds and peeked out at the pool.

By now, night had fallen. Stars twinkled in the sky. The water in the pool was a deep, dark blue. *Wow*, Ash thought, *what a beautiful sight*.

"Look at all those Quagsire!" Misty whispered.

"I wonder if this is where they live," Ash said.

Brock frowned. "But Officer Jenny said they live at Blue Moon Falls. I don't see any falls around here."

"Me, neither." Ash looked around. He didn't see any falls. But he did see exactly what he was looking for. One of the Quagsire was holding the GS Ball!

"There it is! That's the one!" Ash grabbed a Poké Ball and got ready to throw it.

Misty looked alarmed. "Officer Jenny told you to leave those Quagsire alone!"

"Oh, yeah," Ash said. "But . . . " How could he just stand there and do nothing when that Quagsire had Professor Oak's GS Ball?

"Hey, what are those Quagsire doing?"

Misty asked. They all stared at the sky. "They're looking up," said Brock. "They must be waiting for something."

"Up?" Ash asked, looking up himself.

A hot-air balloon floated in the sky above the pool. The white balloon was decorated with the face of a Meowth.

Ash knew that balloon. It belonged to Team Rocket. Jessie, James, and their Pokémon, Meowth, were Pokémon thieves. Right now, it looked like Team Rocket was out to capture the Quagsire. Two long, metal arms stuck out from the basket of Team Rocket's balloon. Each arm had a claw at the end of it for grabbing things.

"Quagsire!" Ash shouted. But he was too late. The thieves used a claw to scoop up a Quagsire. They dangled it over the water.

"What's going on here?" Brock asked. Team Rocket was ready with their motto. "Prepare for trouble," said Jessie. The girl had long red hair that matched the R emblazoned on her white Team Rocket uniform.

"And make it double," said James, a boy with purple hair.

Jessie, James, and Meowth launched into their motto. Ash tuned out. He had heard it a million times before. Besides, he was too busy watching the Quagsire Team Rocket had captured.

The slick little Pokémon slipped out of the clamp. It dove back into the water.

"That wasn't supposed to happen," James said.

"What are you guys doing here, anyway?" Misty called up to them.

"What does it look like?" asked Meowth. "We're stealing all the Quagsire, of course."

"And we're trying to get back our Poké Balls," Jessie added. "Those little thieves stole them."

"Yeah, *we're* the only thieves around here," said James.

"Well, you're not doing a very good job," Misty retorted.

Meowth hit a button on a handheld remote control. "We'll see about that!"

The metal arms moved into action. They tried to catch one Quagsire after another. But the Quagsire were too slippery to catch. They leaped and dove right through the claws on the ends of the arms. One Quagsire after another escaped from Team Rocket.

"Knock this off right now," Jessie screamed at her teammates. "Meowth! Begin Plan B!"

Meowth groaned. "We should have started with

Plan B!" The Pokémon pushed another button on the remote-control device.

The button opened a trapdoor on the bottom of the balloon basket. Out came a gigantic net. The Quagsire were too slippery to catch with the metal claws. But their slick skin could not help them to escape from a net.

In a flash, Team Rocket captured all of the Quagsire!

4

Luckiest Of All

"What a catch!" Jessie and James shouted. "If we sell this many Quagsire, we'll be really rich," Jessie said. She knew Quagsire were rare in most parts of the world.

"Yeah, but what about our missing Poké Balls?" James asked. Team Rocket had almost forgotten about them.

Jessie and James looked down from the balloon. The Poké Balls were lying in some grass beside the water. Jessie and James used the grabbing arms to pick them up.

That gave Ash some extra time. He and the others

caught up with the white balloon. "Hey, Team Rocket!" Ash shouted. "Give back the Quagsire!"

"Don't count on it," Meowth answered, chuckling nastily.

James looked down at Ash. "We might even take . . ."

". . . that Pikachu off your hands, too," Jessie finished.

In a flash, James and Jessie lowered the grabbing arms toward Pikachu.

"Pikachu!" Ash yelled.

"*Pika pi!*" The frightened Pokémon tried to run from the metal arms. But Jessie quickly snatched Pikachu with a claw and pulled the Pokémon into the balloon basket.

"We did it," Meowth bragged.

Blam! A big brown rock slammed into Team Rocket's balloon. *Blam! Blam! Blam!* Several more rocks followed the first one.

"Huh?" Team Rocket looked totally confused. They leaned over the side of the balloon basket to see what was happening.

Dozens of slippery blue Quagsire were standing beside the water. They had come to rescue their trapped friends. They were pelting Team Rocket with dozens of rocks!

Ash grinned at the Quagsire. He had to admire their technique. First, they tossed the rocks into the air. Then they aimed jets of water at the rocks, sending them shooting toward Team Rocket's balloon.

"Cool," Ash said. "They're using their Water Gun attacks."

"Meowth!" Jessie shrieked. "Do something!"

"There's nothing to do!" Meowth replied.

Jessie tried pushing buttons and pulling levers. By accident, he opened the clamp that held Pikachu.

"Pika!" The little yellow Pokémon fell out of the sky. Ash ran to catch it. He hugged the Pokémon tightly.

"Are you okay, Pikachu?" Ash asked.

"Pika!" Pikachu looked as good as new. Ash put down Pikachu. He glared up at Team Rocket. "Bulba-saur, I choose you!"

Ash threw a Poké Ball, and a blue-green Grass-type Pokémon sailed out. Bulbasaur had a green plant bulb growing on its back and a determined look on its face.

"Bulbasaur! Razor Leaf!" Ash shouted. Ash and Bulbasaur had been together for a long time. The Grass-type Pokémon was well trained. It shot dozens of razor-sharp leaves from its plant bulb. The leaves whizzed straight for the net where the Quagsire were trapped. Their sharp edges sliced through the net. The Quagsire were free!

Then one Quagsire took aim. It tossed an extra-large rock into the air and launched it at Team Rocket's balloon.

Direct hit! The rock made a huge hole in the middle of the balloon. A jet of air blew out of the hole. The balloon went totally out of control. It twisted and turned through the sky as all the air leaked out of it.

"Team Rocket's blasting off again!" Jessie, James, and Meowth screamed.

"Quag, quag!" The Quagsire held up their precious round objects and looked to the sky. They looked very happy.

Ash felt happy, too. Pikachu was safe — and so were the Quagsire.

"Hey, the Quagsire are going somewhere," Misty said. Ash looked. All the Quagsire had jumped into the water with their objects. They were swimming away.

"So their home is really somewhere else," Ash said. He knew he had to find out where. "Looks like they're headed upstream," Brock pointed out.

"All right, let's follow them!" Ash said. They all ran after the Quagsire. They chased the blue Pokémon upstream until the river emptied into another pool.

Ash had never seen anything quite like it. The pool was surrounded by green trees on top of rocky cliffs. A big waterfall gushed down a cliff into the pool. A bright moon shone in the sky above the waterfall. The moon had an eerie blue glow.

"Blue Moon Falls," Misty whispered.

"So this is where they live," Ash said.

The Quagsire began tossing their round objects in the air. Then they used Water Gun to shoot the objects toward the waterfall.

"Hmm. It looks like they're launching the round objects they've collected up toward the moon," Brock remarked. "They must be performing some kind of ceremony."

"*Quagsire, quagsire,*" the Quagsire chanted.

Just then, the last of the Quagsire stepped up to launch its round object. Ash felt excited. "That's the GS Ball!"

The ball sailed toward the moon. It went higher than all the others.

The GS Ball splashed into the water. It began floating downstream with the other round objects.

"Wait! Somebody stop that GS Ball!" Ash couldn't let it get away again. He began running downstream as fast as he could.

Brock and Misty followed behind Ash.

The sun was rising as they arrived downstream. It looked like all the people of Cherrygrove City had gathered there. They had come to watch the round objects arrive. They had also come to claim their missing possessions – balls, earrings, yo-yos, marbles, and all sorts of other round things. All of the people looked happy. They were certain the objects would bring them good luck. Officer Jenny was there, too. She reminded people to get out of the water as soon as they had picked up their belongings. A man on the riverbank looked very excited. "Hey! The last one's coming!" he shouted.

Officer Jenny fished out the last round object.

"What's this?" she asked. She held up a gold-and-silver Poké Ball.

Ash raced toward her. He was almost out of breath. "It's, it's mine," he gasped.

Officer Jenny gave the GS Ball to Ash. "Congratulations," she told him. "You got the best luck of all!"

"Huh?" Ash didn't know what she was talking about.

"Your ball came back down the river last. That means it is the luckiest of all the round objects this year," Officer Jenny explained.

"The luckiest of all?" Ash asked. The people of Cherrygrove City began to clap and shout their congratulations to Ash.

Suddenly, Ash felt very happy. "That means all that good luck is mine," he said. "All right! Now I know I'm going to win in the Johto League!"

Pokémon Academy

"Are we anywhere near Violet City?" Ash asked wearily. "We've been walking for days." After getting back the GS Ball from the Quagsire, Ash and his friends headed straight for Violet City and the first gym in the Johto League.

"We'd better hurry up and get there before your luck runs out," Misty teased.

Brock studied a guidebook. "According to this, we're within city limits now. I just can't seem to find the gym."

Ash grabbed the book. "It's got to be here somewhere!"

Ash was so busy looking for the gym that he didn't

notice Pikachu was lagging behind. The little yellow Pokémon had stopped to smell some flowers by the side of the road.

Suddenly, Ash heard a commotion.

"I found it first! It's my Pikachu!" a little boy screamed.

"No, it's mine!" screamed a little girl.

Ash whirled around. A little boy with messy dark hair and a little girl with red ponytails were fighting over his Pikachu. Each child was tugging on one of Pikachu's arms.

"Pika, pika, pikachu!" Pikachu was very upset. Angry sparks danced on its rosy cheeks. Ash knew what that meant.

"Pikachu, wait!" Ash ran to Pikachu and yanked it away from the boy and girl just in time to save them from an electric shock! As Ash held Pikachu above his head, it released a powerful bolt of electricity.

Ash felt the charge from his head to his toes. He was used to it by now, but it still made his hair stand on end.

Finally, the charge died down. "This Pikachu is mine," Ash said weakly.

"Aw, I thought it was a wild Pikachu," the boy said. He did not look grateful to be saved from the shock.

A pretty, dark haired young woman ran up to Ash and the kids. "You can't just leave school like that," she scolded the boy and girl. The woman turned to Ash. "I'm sorry my students bothered you."

The little boy looked at Ash, Brock, and Misty. "Are you guys Pokémon Trainers?"

Ash couldn't help but feel proud. "Yeah."

"Wow!" the little girl said.

"Please, show us your Pokémon," said the little boy.

Both kids looked very excited. So did their teacher. She introduced herself as Miss Priscilla. She explained that she worked at the Pokémon Academy — a school that teaches Pokémon basics to children who want to be Trainers. The little boy and girl — Zack and Lizzie — were two of her students.

"Those children must be so happy to have a teacher as charming as you!" Brock gushed. "I'm Brock, the Pokémon breeder."

Brock pointed to Ash and Misty. "Those two are Ash and Misty. I'm sure they'd love to follow you to your school and show the kids their Pokémon."

Ash's and Misty's eyes popped open wide. They had

no such plans, of course. All Ash wanted was to find the Violet City Gym. But the next thing he knew, he was on the school playground. Then he, Misty, and Brock let their Pokémon out of their Poké Balls.

The playground looked like a great place for children and Pokémon to play. Green trees surrounded the grassy field. It even had a pool for Water-type Pokémon to play in.

Brock pointed at a tall building in the distance. "What's that tower?" he asked.

The teacher smiled. "Why, that's the Sprout Tower."

"Why is it called the Sprout Tower?" Misty asked.

Miss Priscilla explained, "That whole tower is supported by one beam. The beam drifts back and forth like a Bellsprout. That's how the tower got its name."

Ash knew what a Bellsprout was. The combination Grass- and Poison-type Pokémon had a flower bell for a head and a long, thin stem for a body. The stem swayed back and forth. But Ash didn't understand how a tower could work the same way. "If the beam sways, wouldn't the tower move, too?" he asked.

"Seeing is believing," Miss Priscilla assured him. She offered to take Ash and the others on a tour of the tower.

Of course, Brock accepted her offer immediately. Ash wanted to see the tower, too. But first, he had to deal with Zack.

The stubborn little boy still wanted to "capture" Pikachu. While the other kids played, Zack tried to lure Pikachu away from Ash. Naturally, Pikachu wasn't interested.

But little Zack wouldn't give up. He tackled Pikachu and pinned it to the ground. Finally, Pikachu had had enough. The Electric-type Pokémon blasted Zack with a Thundershock.

Ash raced over to Pikachu and Zack. "Stop it, Pikachu!" he shouted.

Ash didn't really blame Pikachu. Zack was acting like a total brat. Still, a good Trainer couldn't let his Pokémon shock younger kids.

Even a shock didn't discourage Zack. "I want Pikachu!" Zack cried.

Ash sighed. "Zack, Pikachu is mine. You can't catch another Trainer's Pokémon."

Zack didn't give up. He grabbed a Poké Ball from his belt and ran after the little yellow Pokémon.

"I'm gonna catch you, Pikachu!" Zack yelled.

Pikachu couldn't take any more. It ran off into some woods near the playground to escape Zack. But bratty Zack chased after Pikachu.

"I'd better go after that kid, anyway." Ash called his other Pokémon back to their Poké Balls.

"We'll go on to see the Sprout Tower," Misty said.

"Okay," Ash agreed. "I'll be there soon and I'll bring Zack and Pikachu with me."

In the woods, Ash caught up to Zack. The boy had his eye on Pikachu. Pikachu's ears were sticking up from behind a bush.

"There you are! Go, Poké Ball!" Zack threw his Poké Ball in Pikachu's direction. The Poké Ball opened up and disappeared behind the bush. A red light flashed. Zack began to jump up and down in triumph. "I did it! I did it!" he screamed. "I caught a Pikachu!"

No way, Ash said to himself. *He couldn't have.* Pikachu hated to be inside a Poké Ball. An inexperienced kid couldn't possibly catch the yellow Pokémon. But Pikachu was nowhere to be seen.

Zack picked up the Poké Ball.

"This Pikachu is mine now! I caught it!" He waved the Poké Ball in the air and did a victory dance. Then he tried to run off with it.

"Zack! Stop right there!" Ash shouted. Something didn't look right about the patch of grass in front of them.

Ash reached out to grab Zack. But it was too late. Someone had set a booby trap. Ash and Zack crashed through a grassy trapdoor and fell down into a deep hole!

"Ouch!" Ash yelled. "What was that? What's going on?" Looking up, Ash got his answer. Jessie, James, and Meowth were staring into the hole. Team Rocket was up to its usual dirty tricks!

"That pitfall plan works every time," Jessie said. She laughed meanly.

"It'll keep them tucked in nice and cozy," James said.

"And it's low budget, too," Meowth added. Ash didn't have to guess what Team Rocket was after. James grinned at Zack.

"Well, kid," James said. "Thanks for catching Pikachu for us."

Jessie leaned into the hole. "Give the Poké Ball to the nice lady," she told Zack.

"Nice lady?" Meowth asked. "Where?"

Jessie smacked Meowth. "I'm the nice lady. So come on and be a good little boy," she told Zack.

Zack glared at Team Rocket. "No way. This is my Pokémon." Suddenly, Zack threw the Poké Ball with all his might. "Go, Pikachu! Get those guys."

The Poké Ball whizzed through the air. A small, friendly-looking Pokémon appeared. It looked kind of like a flower. It had a green stem for a body. Its head was yellow and shaped like a bell. The Pokémon swayed gently back and forth.

Zack's mouth fell open. He stared at the Pokémon in shock. "But that's . . . " he mumbled.

"*Bellsprout*," said the Pokémon.

Bellsprout

"A Bellsprout?" James said.

Team Rocket was very confused. They'd been expecting Pikachu.

"Pikachu must still be hiding somewhere around here," Meowth pointed out.

The next thing Ash knew, Jessie, James, and Meowth were up in a tree. They held red-and-white devices that looked like megaphones. But these devices weren't the kind of megaphones that made voices louder. They were built to make Team Rocket sound like Ash!

Jessie held her device to her mouth. "Help me, Pikachu!" she cried.

Next it was James's turn. "Team Rocket caught me," he whimpered.

"Hurry out and save me! *Meowth!*" Meowth said.

Seconds later, the yellow Pokémon hopped out from behind some bushes. It looked around and began following the sound of the phony voices.

"It fell for it!" Meowth said proudly.

James spoke into his voice device. "I'm down in the hole!"

Pikachu hopped toward the edge of the hole. Meowth spoke into its voice disguiser. "Just a little closer."

Pikachu moved closer and closer to the edge of the hole. Suddenly, Jessie shouted, "Now!" She, James, and Meowth hoisted a giant net above their heads and threw it toward the hole.

"Above you! Dodge!" Ash yelled to Pikachu.

"Pika!" Just in time, Pikachu jumped out of the way of the net. Half of the net fell down into the hole. The rest of it fell on the ground beside the hole.

Ash grabbed the part of the net that dangled into the hole. He and Zack used the net to climb out.

Ash ran to Pikachu and scooped it up in his arms. "You know when you hear my real voice, don't you, Pikachu?"

"Pika, pika," Pikachu agreed.

Up in the tree, Team Rocket wasn't ready to give up. "Catch them all!" Jessie shouted.

"Throw a net!" Meowth added. Then it remembered,

"We're all out of nets!"

Ash had an idea. He tossed Pikachu into a tree, right next to the one Team Rocket was in. "Pikachu, Thunderbolt!"

Pikachu quickly launched a powerful Thunderbolt attack. Giant bolts of lightning shot through the trees. The attack blasted Jessie, James, and Meowth right off their tree branches. They sailed into the sky – and crashed right through the walls of the Sprout Tower!

Miss Priscilla was giving a tour. Misty, Brock, and the kids from the Pokémon Academy were all there. They had gathered in a big open room with a high ceiling and a wide-planked wood floor.

A strange wooden support beam ran through the center of the room. The beam moved slowly back and forth, like a pendulum.

"It's true," Brock observed. "This movement does remind me of a Bellsprout."

"There's one more reason this tower is called Sprout Tower," Miss Priscilla told Brock and Misty.

"What's that?" Brock asked

Miss Priscilla explained, "All Trainers aspiring to the Johto League stop by this tower, and think back on

when they left their hometowns."

"I get it!" Misty said. "They remember that they're young and just starting out themselves – like sprouts."

One floor up, three sets of ears pricked up. Team Rocket saw their chance to get revenge on Ash.

"This time, nothing will stop us!" Meowth vowed.

7

Trouble in the Tower

"Sprout, sprout!" chirped the yellow Flower Pokémon. Ash and Zack were finally on their way to Sprout Tower.

Bellsprout chattered happily and swayed from side to side as they walked down the road. Ash thought it was kind of cute. But Zack was convinced that Bellsprout was mocking him. "Quit imitating me!" he shouted at it, shaking his fists in the air.

"Bellsprout." Now the poor little Pokémon looked worried and confused.

Ash knew he had to say something. "Look, Zack, it might have been an accident, but you did catch that Bellsprout. It's your Pokémon now."

"I don't like Bellsprout," Zack grumbled.

"Why not?" Ash asked. "It's cute."

"I want a Pikachu," Zack insisted. He opened his mouth wide and began to wail. Tears flew from his eyes.

"Bellsprout, sprout, sprout." The Pokémon did its best to cheer up Zack. The little boy looked at Bellsprout. In spite of himself, he began to giggle.

All of a sudden, Pikachu cried out in alarm. *"Pika, pikachu!"*

Pikachu pointed into the distance. Huge black clouds of smoke billowed out of a building in front of them.

"It's the Sprout Tower!" Zack shouted. "It's on fire!"

"Brock and Misty are in there!" Ash cried. "I've got to do something."

Ash and Zack raced toward the tower. Ash saw with relief that his friends were already running out the door. Miss Priscilla and her students were escaping, too.

"Misty! Brock! Is everyone okay?" Ash asked breathlessly.

"We're fine," Misty replied.

Ash grabbed a Poké Ball and threw it as hard as he could. "Squirtle, I choose you!"

Squirtle faced the tower and got ready for action.

"Water Gun!" Ash shouted. Squirtle opened its mouth and blasted the smoking tower with huge jets of water.

That's when Brock spotted something through the smoke. "This is no fire, Ash!" he announced.

Looking up, Ash could see three shadowy figures — Team Rocket! They stood high on a ledge of Sprout Tower.

Weezing, Team Rocket's Poison-type Pokémon, floated alongside them. Weezing looked like a purple cloud with two heads. It had a serious Smoke Screen attack. Ash knew that the smoke was coming from Weezing, not from any fire.

Jessie tossed back her long red hair. "Sprout Tower has now been taken over by Team Rocket!"

They crashed through a window and disappeared inside.

Ash and the others raced into Sprout Tower.

"The beam!" Misty shouted in horror.

Team Rocket chuckled evilly. The wooden beam was still drifting back and forth. But now Weezing was clinging to it. So were two more of Team Rocket's Pokémon.

Arbok was a big purple Cobra Pokémon. It had wound its long body around the beam. It held one end of a saw in its mouth.

Lickitung, a pink Pokémon, had wrapped its long

tongue around the other end of the saw. Weezing floated next to Lickitung, helping it to hold the saw. They worked with Arbok to pull the saw back and forth across the beam. With each pull, the teeth of the saw sliced deeper into the wood.

Meowth held up a remote-control unit and pointed to the beam. A big white rocket with a red R on the front was lashed to the beam with a thick rope.

"Don't make a move, or I'll press this button!" Meowth warned. "And blast off!"

Jessie grinned an evil grin. "If you want to save the tower, hand over Pikachu."

"Not likely!" Ash barked.

"Even if it means the end of this tower?" Meowth asked.

Pikachu stepped toward Jessie. *"Pika,"* it said, hanging its head sadly.

"Pikachu!" Ash yelled.

"Pika." Pikachu looked back at Ash. Jessie scooped up the little Pokémon.

"You're a lot smarter than that twerp Trainer of yours," she said.

Instantly, Pikachu blasted Jessie with its Thunder-

shock attack. But Jessie just laughed. "We thought you might try that, so we came prepared with shockproof rubber boots and gloves."

"We're Pika-proof," Meowth said proudly. Jessie set Pikachu down on the floor. James began wrapping a long rope around and around its body. "We caught it! We caught it!" he shouted gleefully.

Jessie turned to Ash. "Look on the bright side, Ash. Now that we have Pikachu, we won't be bothering you losers anymore!"

Zack looked up at Ash. "Aren't you going to do something?"

"Of course," Ash replied.

Meowth laughed meanly. "You need a lot more experience before you can beat pros like Team Rocket.

You're just like this tower. You're just a little sprout!"

Ash had heard enough. "What's wrong with being a sprout?" Ash yelled back. "Sprouts sprout into flowers, you know!"

"Yeah, that's right!" Zack added.

"Sprout, sprout!" Bellsprout tugged at Zack's sleeve.

Zack glanced at his Pokémon. Suddenly, his eyes lit up. "Bellsprout — that's it. Use Razor Leaf!"

Bellsprout raced toward Meowth. It shot a razor-sharp green leaf at the remote control unit in Meowth's paw. *Zip!* The razor leaf struck the remote and sent it flying.

"Bulbasaur!" Ash shouted. "Get the remote!" Bulbasaur whipped out a long, skinny vine. It used the vine to snag the remote.

"All right!" Ash shouted.

Then James turned to the Pokémon that were still sawing the support beam. "Weezing! Lickitung! A little more!" The Pokémon sawed as hard as they could. The beam was ready to snap at any second.

"Bellsprout! Razor Leaf!" Zack shouted. Bellsprout shot two lethal green leaves at Weezing and Lickitung. The two Pokémon were forced to let go of the saw and leap away from the support beam.

Jessie and James grabbed their Poké Balls and ordered their Pokémon to return. Then they picked up Pikachu, who was still tied up with rope. They raced to the rocket and climbed aboard.

Meowth banged open a panel on the side of the rocket. "Even without the remote, I can launch the rocket with the manual controls," it explained, chuckling.

Ash knew he had to move fast. The rocket was still attached to the beam. If Team Rocket got away, they'd take the beam with them – and destroy the tower in the process. And Pikachu would be gone forever.

"Bulbasaur! Use Razor Leaf to cut Pikachu's rope!" Ash yelled.

Quickly, Bulbasaur let fly one sharp green leaf. It hit its mark, slicing through Pikachu's rope. Pikachu sailed through the air, right into Ash's arms.

Meanwhile, Zack tried to save the beam. "Bellsprout, you use Razor Leaf, too!"

Quickly, Bellsprout shot out a stream of razor leaves. The leaves sliced through the ropes that tied the rocket to the beam. The rocket took off, jetting wildly around the room. Team Rocket screamed as they hung on for dear life. The rocket sailed through a window and into the clear blue sky. "Looks like Team Rocket's blasting off again!"

The beam swayed back and forth, just as it always had. The tower was safe.

Ash congratulated Zack. "Good job, Zack!" Together, the two boys and their Pokémon had defeated Team Rocket, saved the tower, and rescued Pikachu.

"Thanks!" Zack replied, grinning broadly. He turned to Bellsprout and gave it a huge hug. "You were great, Bellsprout!"

Ash, Misty, and Brock walked Miss Priscilla and her students back to their school. Miss Priscilla was very grateful to Ash and the others. But it was time for Ash to move on.

"I'll be really good with my Bellsprout next time we meet, Ash," Zack promised.

"Where to now, Ash?" Misty asked.

Ash grinned. "I can't wait another minute. Let's go to the Violet City Gym. I'm going to earn my first Johto League badge!"

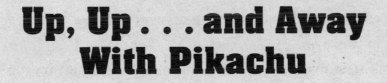

8

Up, Up . . . and Away
With Pikachu

Ash couldn't contain his excitement as they approached
the gym. The tall building rose up in front of him like a
skyscraper.

"I've waited so long for my first battle in the Johto
League," Ash said. "This is going to be great!"

"Pika, pika!" Pikachu was excited, too.

A young man and woman stood behind a counter
at the gym entrance. The pair were wearing matching
white shirts, black bow ties, and horn-rimmed glasses.
They looked very official.

The woman spoke first. "Judging from the looks of you twerps — I mean kids — you must be here to challenge the Violet City Gym."

"If so," the man added, "we must inspect your Pokémon first."

"Inspect my Pokémon?" Ash asked. He had never had this happen before.

"What exactly are you?" Misty asked.

"We're official Pokémon inspectors," the woman replied. "Pokémon must be of a certain level to battle in this gym."

The man grabbed Pikachu and set it down on the counter. "We'll start with this Pikachu."

"Ooh, this Pikachu doesn't cut it!" said the woman.

"It's nothing but problems from head to tail!" the man agreed.

"We'll just take it off your hands!" the woman announced. She scooped up Pikachu in her arms and turned away from Ash. The man followed at her heels. They ran down the street.

"Hey, wait!" Ash shouted after them.

Just then, a hot-air balloon descended to the sidewalk. The balloon had a Meowth face painted on it.

"Oh, no!" Ash cried. "Not again."

Jessie and James climbed into the balloon, taking Pikachu with them.

Jessie placed Pikachu inside a glass container. Sparks flew from Pikachu's body as it tried to shock her, but the glass protected her from its attacks.

"Give me back my Pikachu!" Ash demanded.

"Hey, what's that?" Misty said, pointing at the sky. A large, winged figure sailed toward the hot-air balloon.

"Is it a Flying-type Pokémon?" Ash wondered.

Brock shook his head. "No. Look more closely. That's a hang glider."

The hang glider's pilot was a stern-faced man with thick black hair. He wore a long white robe with a black belt. A round Pokémon that looked like an owl was perched on the man's shoulder. Ash recognized the Pokémon − a Hoothoot. He had met one on one of his first adventures in the West.

"Go, Hoothoot!" the man shouted. The Owl Pokémon flapped its wings and flew toward Team Rocket's balloon basket. Hoothoot swooped in close and snatched Pikachu in its glass container right out of Jessie's hands!

A Mysterious Rescue

"Good work, Hoothoot!" the man in the hang glider said.

Jessie, James, and Meowth looked furious. "Give back Pikachu!" they screeched.

Ash didn't know whether to be grateful or scared. "What's he doing with my Pikachu?"

Ash and his friends stared up at the glider. "They're coming this way," Ash observed.

"They might just be bringing Pikachu back," Brock said hopefully.

Up in the balloon basket, Jessie was fuming. "No fair! You can't steal Pikachu. We stole it first!" she shrieked. "Arbok, shred that glider's wings with Poison

Sting." The huge Pokémon rose up in the balloon basket. It opened its mouth wide. Tiny daggers of venom shot out. They whistled toward the glider and slashed its wings in dozens of places.

"We did it!" cheered Meowth.

The pilot was forced to abandon his glider. He fell toward the ground, still clutching the glass container that held Pikachu. For a second, they both looked like goners. Then the man managed to pull a Poké Ball from his robe. "Go!" he shouted, throwing the ball.

A huge, Bird Pokémon appeared.

"A Pidgeot?" Ash asked.

The Pokémon flapped its giant wings and dipped under the man. Holding Pikachu, the man climbed to safety on the Pidgeot's back. Jessie wasn't about to give up. "Arbok, Poison Sting!" she commanded. More poison darts shot out of Arbok's mouth.

"Spin and Evade!" the man shouted.

Pidgeot ducked the attack.

"Pidgeot! Hit the balloon with your wings!" the man cried.

The fearsome Pokémon raced toward Team Rocket. With one swipe of its powerful wings, it slashed a huge

hole in Team Rocket's balloon.

"Our turn can't be over already!" James complained.

But their balloon spun away through the sky as all the air rushed out of it.

"Looks like Team Rocket's blasting off again!" they screeched.

The Pidgeot glided smoothly to the ground. The man hopped off its back and handed Pikachu to Ash. "I believe this is yours."

"Thanks!" Ash said. He stroked Pikachu's head. "Are you hurt, Pikachu?"

"Pika!" Ash could tell that Pikachu was fine, now that it was safe with him again.

Misty looked at the man and his Pokémon in awe.

"That Pidgeot is so big!"

"It's much bigger than the one I used to have," Ash chimed in.

At that, the man's eyes lit up. "What? You had a Pidgeot, too?"

"Yeah," Ash replied. "Some things came up and I had to leave it in the forest near my hometown. I'll never forget riding over the forest on its back," he said.

"I'm sure you won't," the man replied. "Pidgeot are the best Flying-type Pokémon."

The man stepped toward Ash and clapped his hand on Ash's shoulder. "I can tell we'll get along," he said solemnly.

Ash held out his hand. "I'm Ash Ketchum from Pallet Town. Nice to meet you!"

The man took Ash's hand and shook it firmly. "I'm Falkner," he said. "Leader of the Violet Gym."

10

Chikorita vs. Hoothoot

"You're the Violet Gym Leader?" Ash asked, shocked. He would have to battle this guy for his first Johto League gym badge.

Falkner seemed just as surprised. He led Ash and his friends into the tall gym tower. They rode an elevator all the way to the top. The elevator dropped them off in a large open arena on the roof of the tower. "Welcome to my gym, Ash," Falkner said.

Hmmm, open air. Great place for Flying-type Pokémon to battle, Ash realized. He walked to one end of the battle area and faced Falkner.

A judge in a white robe walked to the middle of the

arena. "The official battle between the Gym Leader, Falkner, and the challenger from Pallet Town, Ash, will now begin. Each will use three Pokémon."

"I'll show you how powerful Flying-type Pokémon truly are!" The gym leader hurled a Poké Ball, choosing Hoothoot.

Ash cocked his arm and threw his first Poké Ball. "Chikorita, I choose you!"

"*Chika.*" The pale green Pokémon sailed out of its ball.

Falkner was surprised by Ash's choice. "You should know that Grass-type Pokémon are weak against Flying-type Pokémon. It's hard to believe you ever had a Pidgeot."

"My Pokémon know how to work together," Ash said boldly. "It doesn't matter what type we face."

The judge gave the signal to begin. Falkner let Ash make the first move. "Chikorita! Vine Whip!" Ash yelled.

"*Chika!*" Two green vines shot forth from Chikorita's neck. The Grass-type Pokémon used them to flail at Hoothoot.

"Hoothoot, to the skies!"

The Flying-type Pokémon flew upward. In seconds, it was beyond the reach of Chikorita's Vine Whips.

"Don't let it get away, Chikorita!" Ash commanded. "Use Vine Whip once more."

Chikorita sailed forward toward Hoothoot, its vines ready to strike.

"Hoothoot, to the sky!" The Owl Pokémon soared high and then swooped down at Chikorita.

"Hoothoot! Move right into Peck attack!" Falkner shouted. The Flying-type Pokémon flew at Chikorita. Over and over, it used its hard, sharp beak to peck at Chikorita's head.

"Chikorita! Fight back with Razor Leaf!"

"*Chika!*" Chikorita reared back and tossed its head at the pecking Pokémon. Three razor-sharp leaves zoomed toward Hoothoot.

"Hoothoot! Climb!" Falkner yelled. Hoothoot flapped its wings. It backed up, up, and away into the sky. The razor leaves flew beneath it.

"Now dive!" Falkner continued. "Tackle at highest speed!"

"*Hoothoot!*" The Flying-type Pokémon soared toward Chikorita. *Wham!* Hoothoot divebombed Chikorita. It slammed the light green Pokémon with its beak, then flew away.

Hoothoot made a sharp turn in the air. It flew straight at Chikorita's head again. "Look out, Chikorita!" Ash shouted. "Fight back with Vine Whip!"

"*Chika.*" Chikorita sailed through the air toward Hoothoot. It lashed out with its Vine Whips. But Hoothoot was just too much for little Chikorita. *Bam!* Once again, Hoothoot slammed into Chikorita's head with its beak. The Grass-type Pokémon fell to the ground, bounced a few times, then lay still.

"Chikorita!" Ash ran to his Pokémon. The judge announced his ruling. "Chikorita is unable to battle! Hoothoot wins!"

Pikachu vs. Dodrio

Ash was stunned by the loss. Still, Chikorita had tried its best. And Ash had two Pokémon left. He returned Chikorita to its Poké Ball. "Thank you, Chikorita. Take a nice, long rest."

"Chikorita was no match for an attack from the sky," Falkner said smugly.

Just you wait, Ash thought. He turned to Pikachu. "You're next. I'm counting on you."

"Pika, pikachu!" Ash could see that Pikachu was eager to battle. Sparks crackled above its rosy cheeks.

The judge banged a drum to start the second round. "Begin!"

"Make the first move, Hoothoot! Tackle!" Falkner shouted.

Hoothoot soared through the air toward Pikachu. It was going to divebomb Pikachu just like it had done to Chikorita.

But Ash had other plans. "Pikachu! Use Agility to confuse it!"

"*Pika!*" The Electric-type Pokémon stretched out its arms and flew at Hoothoot. *Zip!* Pikachu suddenly turned and shot off in the opposite direction. It ran to the left, then shot to the right.

Hoothoot was totally confused. It tried hard, but it could not tackle speedy Pikachu. Pikachu faced Hoothoot again. Sparks began to fly from its face.

Falkner's face went pale. "This is bad. Climb, Hoot-hoot!"

Hoothoot headed for the sky. It flew higher and higher – but not high enough to escape Pikachu.

"Now! Thunderbolt!" Ash yelled.

"Pika!" Pikachu launched a mighty Thunderbolt. A gigantic spear of lightning shot high into the sky. It climbed all the way to where Hoothoot was fluttering. *Zap!* The lightning bolt fried the Flying-type Pokémon.

"Hoothoot . . ." Hoothoot tumbled from the sky and bounced on the ground.

The judge ruled. "Hoothoot is unable to battle. Pikachu wins."

Ash was surprised by Falkner's choice for the next round. Dodrio was a fuzzy orange Triple Bird Pokémon with three heads. Each head had a long, pointy beak.

But Dodrio had one big drawback. "I thought Dodrio couldn't fly," Ash said.

"My Dodrio can," Falkner assured him.

Ash gulped. A flying Dodrio? He'd been sure there was no such thing. This match might be tougher than he'd thought.

The judge banged the drum. "Begin!"

"I'll give you the first move," Falkner said. "My Dodrio can handle it."

Ash planned his strategy. "Okay, Pikachu! Agility once more!"

"Pika!" Pikachu took off running. It leaped into the air.

"We'll use Agility, too!" shouted Falkner. Dodrio raced at Pikachu and jumped up high. Pikachu darted left, then it shot right. It went forward and then back. Dodrio did the same thing.

"Their Agility attacks match up perfectly," Brock said.

"But no one will win if this keeps up," Misty pointed out.

"Togi," her Togepi agreed.

Ash knew it was time for a new move. "Pikachu, find your target and then use Thunderbolt," he called out.

"*Pika.*" Pikachu aimed itself at Dodrio. Then it lit up the field with electric energy as it launched a Thunderbolt attack.

"That's what I've been waiting for," Falkner said. "Fly, Dodrio!"

"*Dodrio.*" Dodrio took a flying leap. It soared right over Pikachu's Thunderbolt.

"Oh, I get It," Brock said from the sidelines. "When Falkner said Dodrio could fly, he just meant it could jump really high!"

"Dodrio, Fury attack!" Falkner shouted.

"*Dodrio!*" The Pokémon swooped out of the sky and aimed its three beaks at Pikachu.

"Flatten it now!" Falkner screamed.

"*Pika!*" The trembling little yellow Electric-type Pokémon backed away in fear.

"Dodrio! Drill Peck!"

"*Dodrio.*" Dodrio launched itself at Pikachu again. This time its three beaks were spinning like drill bits.

"Pikachu!" Ash, Misty, and Brock all screamed.

"Pikaaaaa!" The little Pokémon leaped backward, away from Dodrio.

"This match is mine!" Falkner shouted, "Dodrio, stop it with Tri attack!"

Once again, Dodrio sailed toward Pikachu. Its three mouths were open. Its three tongues were vibrating. It made a horrible squealing sound.

Suddenly, Ash knew what to do. If Dodrio could fly, then so could Pikachu.

"Don't give in, Pikachu! Fight Jump with Jump!" Ash called out.

Pikachu sprang into the air. It landed on Dodrio's heads and bounced off them.

"Now, Pikachu. Drop Thunder on them!" Ash yelled.

"Pika!" said Pikachu jumping again. From above, Pikachu hit Dodrio with a powerful Thunderbolt.

"Dodrio," said all three heads weakly. Dodrio fell over in a faint.

Dodrio was tough. It opened its eyes and tried to stand up. Dodrio just couldn't do it. It collapsed in a heap.

"Dodrio is unable to battle," said the judge. "Pikachu wins!"

"We did it!" Ash cheered.

"Dodrio, you showed plenty of spunk!" Falkner said. "Take a rest."

Ash had a pretty good idea what Pokémon Falkner would choose next. Sure enough, the gym leader chose his huge, powerful Pidgeot.

Pikachu looked really tired. "Do you need a rest?" Ash asked.

"Pika!" The Pokémon shook its head and leaped to its feet. Ash could tell that it wanted to keep fighting.

"Begin!" the judge ordered.

"Decide this match quickly, Pikachu!" Ash encouraged it. "Thunderbolt!"

Pikachu leaped high in the air. With all its might, it unleashed a Thunderbolt as high as it could.

"Fly, Pidgeot!"

"Pidgeot!" The Flying-type Pokémon soared above Pikachu's Thunderbolt, then returned to its place at Falkner's side.

"Pidgeot, Whirlwind!" The big Bird Pokémon shot straight up. It flapped its wings as hard as it could, creating a tornado-like wind. Pikachu tried to respond with a Thunderbolt, but it had no more energy. The Whirlwind blew Pikachu to the ground. It rolled to a stop and fainted.

"Pikachu!" Ash ran to its side.

The judge ruled, "Pikachu is unable to battle. Pidgeot wins."

"Good work, Pikachu," Ash told it. Losing Pikachu was quite a blow. But Ash could use one more Pokémon in this battle. He threw out a Poké Ball.

"Charizard, I choose you!"

12

Final Round

"Charizard last, huh? There's a worthy opponent." Falkner was impressed by Ash's choice.

Charizard got ready for battle. The second evolution of Charmander, it was a large Pokémon with an awesome Flamethrower attack. A burning ember glowed at the end of its long tail. Best of all, Charizard could fly. That would be important in a battle against Pidgeot.

The judge beat the drum to begin the final round.

"Pidgeot, fly!"

"You, too, Charizard!"

The two huge Pokémon flew at each other.

"Charizard, Flamethrower!" The Flame Pokémon opened its mouth wide and blew a sizzling orange flame at Pidgeot.

"Pidgeot! Barrel Roll and Evade!" The Bird Pokémon tilted to one side and rolled away from the attack.

"Charizard, keep going with Flamethrower!" Charizard soared after Pidgeot. It breathed a steady stream of fire.

"Pidgeot, Agility!" The Flying-type Pokémon darted away from Charizard and zipped from side to side. Its speed was truly amazing.

"Use Flamethrower again!" Ash yelled.

Charizard flew at Pidgeot and breathed another blast of fire.

"Pidgeot, Whirlwind!"

Pidgeot reared back and beat its wings. It blew the flame right back in Charizard's face. Charizard fell to the ground.

"Charizard! Are you okay?" Charizard struggled to its feet. It tried to lift off.

Pidgeot sped toward Charizard. Ash tried to decide what to do next. Fire attacks were no good – Pidgeot would just blow them back at Charizard.

"Fly and return!" Ash shouted.

Charizard tried to take off. But something was wrong with its wing. It must have been injured in the fall. Charizard tried to flap it and wound up falling over. Pidgeot raced toward the fallen Pokémon.

"Stand up, Charizard!" Ash screamed.

Charizard had to get out of Pidgeot's way.

Falkner thought he saw his chance to win. "Pidgeot! Finish it off now! Quick attack!"

The massive Bird Pokémon zoomed toward Charizard. Once again, it knocked Charizard to the ground.

"Ash!" Brock shouted. "If you don't do something fast, Charizard's gonna get it!"

Falkner had a suggestion. "You could forfeit the match."

That wasn't exactly what Ash had in mind. "What? No way!"

Falkner gave Ash a firm lecture. "It's a Trainer's duty to protect his Pokémon when they are unable to keep battling. Your Charizard can't even fly."

"My Charizard's not ready to quit. It can battle even if it can't fly!" Ash said boldly.

"Char." Charizard bravely got to its feet, as if to prove that Ash was right.

Falkner shrugged. "Maybe this defeat will teach you a lesson."

Falkner turned to his Pokémon. "Pidgeot! Quick attack at your highest speed!"

Pidgeot raced toward Charizard. Despite what he had said, Ash knew Charizard was in trouble if it couldn't get off the ground. "Come on, Charizard, fly! You're the most stubborn Pokémon I've got. You're not going to get beaten, are you?"

Ash's words sparked something in Charizard. Charizard flapped its wings. Slowly but surely, it rose into the air.

"You did it, Charizard!" Ash shouted.

"It may be able to fly, but I doubt it's got much speed," Falkner said arrogantly. "Pidgeot! Agility!"

Again, Pidgeot showed off its lightning quick Agility moves. There was no way Charizard could catch it. Every time Charizard came close, Pidgeot would dart behind it.

Falkner grinned confidently. "Try as you might, nothing's going to change. Charizard's moves will never be as fast as Pidgeot's," he said.

Nothing's going to change . . . The words struck a chord in Ash's mind. Charizard charged at Pidgeot. And every time, Pidgeot escaped by darting behind Charizard.

Suddenly, Ash knew what to do. "Charizard!" Ash yelled. "Follow Pidgeot." Charizard flew at Pidgeot. As usual, Pidgeot darted behind Charizard. But this time, Ash was ready.

"Charizard, use Fire Spin behind you," Ash said. The flame on the end of Charizard's — glowing tail shot out, scorching Pidgeot. The Pokémon was stunned. It stopped flying and just hung in the air.

"Way to go, Charizard. Now capture Pidgeot and do Seismic Toss!"

Charizard grabbed the immobile Bird Pokémon in a big bear hug. It spun Pidgeot around and around, building speed.

Finally, Charizard used all of its strength to fling Pidgeot through the air.

"Pidgeot!" Falkner screamed, distressed. The Flying-type Pokémon fell to the ground.

The judge made his ruling. "Pidgeot is unable to battle. Ash wins!"

"You did it, Charizard!" Ash shouted.

Falkner congratulated Ash. "I never imagined you'd use Pidgeot's speed to your advantage. That was a beautiful strategy. This Zephyr Badge is yours."

Falkner handed Ash a glittering stone. "Thank you!" Ash looked at the new badge. He was filled with joy. He'd finally earned his first Johto League badge!

"I got a Zephyr Badge," he said, not sure if he believed it. He patted the GS Ball through his backpack. "I guess those Quagsire did bring me good luck.

"Pika," agreed Pikachu.

Falkner smiled. "Battling with you has really inspired me, Ash. Good luck to you in the Johto League."

"Thank you," Ash said. He turned to Brock and Misty. "Come on, let's get going."

"Get going?" Misty asked. "Ash, don't you want to rest? That was a tough battle."

Ash shook his head. "No way," he said. "I've got three more gym badges to earn!"

Next in this series:

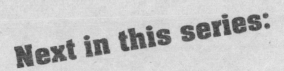

Ash wants to be a great Pokémon Trainer. But sometimes Trainers have to make big sacrifices.

Charizard can only get stronger if it leaves Ash – forever. But that means Ash has no Fire-type Pokémon at all. Have his dreams of becoming a Pokémon Master gone up in flames?